Mo
Has a Problem

Scott Campbell  Eric Hawkins

Text Copyright © 2021 by Scott M. Campbell
Illustrations Copyright © 2021 by Eric K. Hawkins

Any references to historical events, real people, or real places are used fictitiously. Names, characters, and places are products of the author's imagination.

All rights reserved. No part of this book may be reproduced or used in any manner without written permission of the copyright owner except for the use of brief quotations embodied in critical articles and book reviews.

Book cover and book design by Eric Hawkins
The text is set with Rockwell.

First printing edition December 2021

For more information, address:
scottcampbell82@gmail.com

Nickel Leaf Press
1707 Green Hills Drive
Nashville, TN, 37215

ISBN 978-0-578-33993-1 (hardback)

To Sarah, Jed, Carter and Luke
SC

To Jess, Luke, Evie and HK
EH

Hey, Mo!
What's up?

What's happening, Ali?
My back is itching.
It's bothering me.

When mine starts to itch,
I just use a stick.
It fixes it up.
It fixes it quick.

With the length of my arms,
I'm not quite sure how…

Hey Mo, Gotta go!

Okay. Bye for now.

Grrit

Grrump

Grraaw

Grrumm!

Ugh

Humph

Fritz

None.

Hey Mo, How are you?

Hey Imani, I'm fine.

Well, fine is not great.
Say, what's on your mind?

My back itches bad.
It's driving me mad.

No worries my friend.
No need to be sad.

When I have an itch,
I seek out a tree.
In minutes it's gone.
Then I'm back to me.

    Yeah, that sounds good.
    I'll give it a try…

Oh man! Gotta bounce!

    Well, thanks.
    Goodbye!

Arrgh!
Ooocha!
Eheee!
Wow!

Humph!
Ugh!
Fritz!
Ow.

Hey Mo, how's it going?

Camille, I'm alright.
My back's itched all day,
and it's nearly night.

Well, when my back itches,
I roll in the mud
It softens my fur
and gets rid of the crud.

    I'm not fond of dirt,
    but you are like fam.

Bye Mo, need to go!

    Alright. See ya, Cam.

Plop

    Roll

        Squish

           Squirt.

              Humph.

                Ugh.

                Fritz.

                Dirt.

I need a bath.

Wow, that's a lot,
but I have a hack.
Just ask your kids
to scratch that old back!

    Well, kids I don't have,
    but a thought, if you might . . .

Later Mo, time to go!

    Thanks anyway, Raj.
    Have a good night.

Hhhh

Hmmm

Hfff

Sigh.

Ugh

Humph

Fritz

Why?

Hey, Friend.
Why so down?

Liv, don't want to bore.
It's just -
It's just . . .
My back itches.

I've wriggled, rubbed, rolled.
My mind's in a tizzy.

My arms are too short.
My back is too far.

I'm sure I need help,
but my friends are too busy.

Hey Mo...What's that?!

I don't see any . . .

*A friend is present.
A friend will care.
A friend will drop everything
just to be there.*

*A friend doesn't hurry,
is generous with time.
A friend just does
because doing is kind.*

Be kind.

AUTHOR

Scott Campbell makes his debut as a children's picture book author with *Mo Has a Problem*. He is the Executive Director of Persist Nashville Nonprofit and a life-long educator. As a former high school principal and teacher, Scott has developed a passion for creating Social Emotional Learning tools for the classroom. Scott and his wife have three boys.

ILLUSTRATOR

Eric Hawkins is an architect, musician and designer. His architectural projects have received national and local design recognition, ranging in size from small wooden bowls to skyscrapers. Although his passion for drawing began as a child, *Mo Has a Problem* is Eric's first picture book to illustrate. He lives with his wife and three children in Nashville.

CPSIA information can be obtained
at www.ICGtesting.com
Printed in the USA
LVRC081207220122
708508LV00021B/217